Puffin Books

RIDE TO THE RESCUE

Kate is desperate to have her own pony and can't believe it
when her Dad sort-of promises her one. But what with the
wedding, all the excitement of having a new Mum and their
surprise holiday, Kate is sure he's forgotten her.

When they finally reach their secret destination, Kate feels
terribly disappointed, but things soon pick up and it turns out
to be a holiday full of surprises and dramas.

This is a thrilling and fast-moving adventure story.

June Crebbin has been an English teacher for most of her life,
in both primary and secondary schools in Leicestershire and
Yorkshire. June began writing in 1971 while continuing part-
time teaching, and looking after a young family. She now
works part-time in a primary school near Leicester but con-
tinues to write widely for adults and children.

*Also by June Crebbin*

THE JUNGLE SALE

# JUNE CREBBIN

# Ride to the Rescue

### ILLUSTRATED BY CATHERINE BRADBURY

PUFFIN BOOKS

# For Peter and Philip

PUFFIN BOOKS

Published by the Penguin Group
27 Wrights Lane, London W8 5TZ, England
Viking Penguin Inc., 40 West 23rd Street, New York, New York 10010, USA
Penguin Books Australia Ltd, Ringwood, Victoria, Australia
Penguin Books Canada Ltd, 2801 John Street, Markham, Ontario, Canada L3R 1B4
Penguin Books (NZ) Ltd, 182–190 Wairau Road, Auckland 10, New Zealand

Penguin Books Ltd, Registered Offices: Harmondsworth, Middlesex, England

First published by Viking Kestrel 1989
Published in Puffin Books 1990
10 9 8 7 6 5 4 3 2 1

Text copyright © June Crebbin, 1989
Illustrations copyright © Catherine Bradbury, 1989
All rights reserved

Made and printed in Great Britain by
Richard Clay Ltd, Bungay, Suffolk
Filmset in Palatino (Linotron 202)

# 1. *The promise*

Kate went riding every Sunday. She always rode Toffee. He was a fat, brown pony who dreamed along behind the others – but he was not the pony of Kate's dreams.

The pony of Kate's dreams was black, jet-black, as black as coal, as black as midnight. When he moved, his feet barely touched the ground. He seemed almost to fly.

'Catch me up!' yelled Sharon, who was ahead of her.

Kate came down to earth with a bump. She dug her heels into Toffee's fat sides. It was like a fly tickling an elephant. Toffee's slow amble did not falter.

'He won't,' shouted Kate.

Sharon drew her pony back so that they were riding side by side.

'You'll never learn to ride properly if you don't try a different pony,' she said.

One day, thought Kate. One day I'll show you. I'll be riding my own pony soon. Just you wait. That'll surprise you.

But she didn't want to tell Sharon just yet. So she told her something else instead.

'This time tomorrow,' said Kate, 'I'll be on my honeymoon.'

'It's not your honeymoon,' said Sharon. 'It's your mum and dad's.'

'Dad says the honeymoon's for all of us,' said Kate. She could hardly

wait for Eve to become her mum.
She'd never known her real mum who
had died when Kate was only a year
old.

'Do you know where you're going
yet?' said Sharon.

'No,' said Kate. 'It's a big surprise.'

'Is Luke going?'

'Yes,' said Kate. 'We're all going.'

'He'll be your brother, you know,'
said Sharon.

Kate pulled a face. 'I know.'

'For ever and ever,' said Sharon.

'Shut up,' said Kate.

'Till death do you part,' said Sharon.

'I'm not marrying *him*,' said Kate crossly.

'You're not marrying anyone,' said Sharon. 'That's why it's not your honeymoon.'

At the front of the line, Mrs Farmer stood up in her stirrups. 'Prepare to trot,' she shouted, and waved her right arm high in the air like a general about to charge into battle.

'Trot ON!' she yelled.

'See you,' said Sharon. She tightened her reins and kicked Chestnut hard. The pony shot forward.

'You're supposed to squeeze with the calves of your legs,' Kate shouted after her, digging her heels into Toffee's fat sides for all she was worth. 'You're not supposed to kick.'

Toffee obviously thought so too. Though Kate's legs flapped like sails, Toffee walked stolidly on.

One of the girls at the back of the line came forward to help. 'Kick him on,' she said. 'You're holding up the line.'

What do you think I'm doing? thought Kate, peeling a banana?

'I have,' she said aloud. 'He won't go.' She let the reins drop.

Toffee stopped altogether then, hemmed in by the grey pony at his side. Rainbow danced along the path. Even when the girl reined him in to let the other riders pass, Rainbow couldn't keep still. He pawed the ground, he tossed his head in the air,

he pranced on the spot like a circus horse.

'Soon,' Kate promised herself. 'Soon, I'll have a pony like that.'

'Now kick him on,' said the girl. 'He should go now.'

And Toffee did. Suddenly he decided he didn't like being left behind and, besides, the turn in the road meant they were heading for home. He put his head down and set off at a fast lurch down the lane. Kate, taken by surprise, bumped awkwardly in the saddle.

'Up, down, UP, down, UP, down!' chanted the girl at her side.

'Clear off!' said Kate.

'What?'

'We're off!' said Kate.

By the time they had caught up with the line ahead, everyone had slowed down to a walk. But not Toffee. He was heading for home. There was no stopping him now. Straight through the line he went. Straight through the door into the indoor school.

'You shouldn't always ask for Toffee,' said Sharon, as they unsaddled the ponies.

Kate led Toffee away to the stable. She wanted to try a different pony. She wanted to ride Rainbow. All week she thought, I'll ask for Rainbow, but when the time came and they arrived at the stables, she found herself saying, 'I'd like to ride Toffee, please,' just as she always did.

'What about Tommy?' said Sharon, following her. 'He's easy to handle. You could manage him.'

'I won't need to,' said Kate suddenly. 'I'll be getting my own pony soon.'

The words were out before she could stop herself. She hadn't planned to tell Sharon yet. She'd only known herself a few days. She'd wanted to surprise Sharon.

Sharon certainly was surprised. 'When?'

'Soon.'

'For your birthday?'

Kate didn't think so, but . . . 'Maybe,' she said. 'Yes, could be.'

12

The two girls shut the ponies into their stables and carried the saddles and bridles to the tack-room.

'You can't be having a pony,' said Sharon.

'I am,' said Kate. 'Dad said so.'

'What did your father actually say?'

'He said, "Soon you'll be having a pony of your very own."'

Kate was certain those were the exact words because she'd said them over and over to herself so many times since.

'Will you keep him here?' said Sharon. 'Will you let me ride him?'

'You can ride him whenever you want,' said Kate. 'Well,' she added, 'all the time I'm not riding him.'

They waited by the riding-school gates, kicking the gravel, watching for Kate's father.

'What sort of a pony?' said Sharon.

'Black,' said Kate immediately. She saw him at once in her mind's eye. The small neat head, the intelligent, kind eyes. She saw him galloping towards her across the field.

'Have you seen him then?' asked Sharon.

'Yes,' said Kate. Then, 'No, not yet.' Kate saw her father's car coming up the road. 'Don't say I told you. I think Dad wants to keep it a secret.'

But the minute Sharon got into the car, she said, 'Isn't it good news about the pony?'

Kate glared at her.

'What pony?' said Dad. 'Who said anything about a pony?'

'You did, Dad. You know.'

'Me? I don't remember,' said her father.

14

# 2. *Surprises*

The next day, after the wedding, Kate and her family set off on the honeymoon, their first holiday together. It was lovely to be sharing the car with her new mum and brother. Of course, Dad and Kate had shared the car with Eve and Luke before when they had all been on outings together. But now Luke was her brother and Eve was her mum. Now there were four of them all the time – a real family.

'Mum,' said Kate, leaning forwards.

Eve turned.

'Will *you* tell me where we're going?' said Kate.

'No,' said Eve, smiling. 'But you'll like it.'

'Where *are* we going, Dad?' Kate asked for the fourth time.

'Not telling you,' said Dad cheerfully. 'I told you.'

He and Eve smiled at each other.

Kate lapsed back into the seat. It was going to be a long journey, that's all she knew, and she was bored already. She glanced at Luke. He was writing something in a notebook balanced on his knee. His long legs seemed to fill the back of the car.

If she could have chosen, Kate would have preferred a younger brother, or better still, a younger sister. Luke was sixteen. But still, Sharon's older brother was good fun. He always teased her when she went round to play and pretended to punch her. Sometimes he didn't miss. But that was better than being ignored.

Which is what Luke did. He didn't talk to anyone much.

'Dad,' said Kate, leaning forwards again.

'I'm not telling you,' he said.

'No, I'm not talking about that. You know you said I was having a pony. . .'

'Paul!' said Eve. 'You've told her!'

'Not all of it,' said Dad.

'You're hopeless!' she said, but Kate could see that Eve was smiling.

'When?' said Kate, and to make it quite clear she said, 'When am I having my very own pony?'

'It's a surprise,' said Dad. 'Now, don't ask me any more or you'll spoil it.'

Kate sat back. She pulled her legs up on to the seat and hugged her knees. It was true all right. She really was going to have a pony! Her head buzzed with questions. What sort of a pony? Where were they going to get it? And most important of all – when?

Kate liked surprises but she liked them to come all in one piece. Dad always seemed to give them out a bit at a time so that when you finally arrived at the surprise, it wasn't a surprise at all.

I could go mad trying to guess, thought Kate.

'You could guess where we're going if you like,' said Dad from the front seat. 'I'll give you a clue.'

'No, thank you,' said Kate. She wasn't starting that. 'I want it to be a surprise.'

And it was a surprise to find, after their long journey to the coast, that they were crossing the sea to Ireland. During the night they slept on the boat and were up early the next morning to start the final lap of their journey.

They stopped once, in a small

village, to have a meal in what looked like someone's front room. By this time, Kate had decided it was to be a farm holiday. They were travelling through so much countryside.

She would help with everything, she decided, cows, calves, lambs, chickens, even if it meant getting up early in the morning to do so. The more she thought about it, the more she liked the idea.

But when, towards late afternoon, Dad did draw up in front of a farmhouse, the grim stone building and bare farmyard didn't fit in with the picture in Kate's mind at all.

Flat, grey countryside stretched away in every direction, with only a few scraggy trees to break the skyline. The trees in her garden at home were taller and greener than these.

20

'Here we are,' said Dad. 'Out you get!'

Kate did her best to cover her disappointment.

'Is this where we're staying?' she said. 'Is it a farm holiday?'

'No,' said Dad. 'It's a caravan holiday. Out you get!'

And then Kate saw it.

A gypsy caravan, standing in the far corner of the yard with its two harness poles sticking out in front. They were going to travel the countryside like real gypsies.

'With a horse?' said Kate.

'Of course!' said Dad.

'Can I go and look?' Kate was already half-way across the yard.

'Yes,' shouted Dad after her. 'Just look and then come and help carry things.'

It wasn't quite like the gypsy caravans Kate had seen in books. This one was like a huge barrel set on a platform with wheels: and the wheels looked far too small for the top. It was painted two shades of green, light-green and dark-green. There were green check curtains above the half-door at the front and red check curtains across the window at the

back. Inside there was a cooker and a table, two bunks at the back and two long seats on each side, with a space under them to store things.

Kate began to feel excited.

The farmer arrived with Dad.

'You're a bit late starting,' he said. 'You'd best be getting a move on.'

'Right,' said Dad. 'Suitcases first. Everything out and packed under the seats. We'll leave the actual cases in the car.'

'Where's the horse?' said Kate.

'We'll fetch him when we're ready,' said Dad.

'Just come to the door,' said the farmer. 'You'll need feed and halters and maps.'

'I've got maps,' said Dad. 'Thank you all the same.'

'Mine are marked with the routes,'

said the farmer. 'You'll need mine.'

He moved away.

Eve stayed in the caravan, unpacking things from the suitcases as Dad and Luke brought them in – clothes, sleeping-bags, books, games.

Underneath the cooker she found a single drawer containing knives and forks and spoons, and underneath that was a tiny cupboard with cups, plates, saucepans and a kettle.

Kate skipped from the caravan to the car, trying to help carry things but mostly getting in the way. At last it was all done.

'Right, horse next, I think,' said Dad.

The cart-horse was huge. Far bigger than Kate had imagined. His name was Tom. Kate watched her father and the farmer harness him to the caravan and then they were shown where to store the buckets and feed on the hooks at the back of the caravan. A spade hung from one of the hooks.

'What's the spade for?' asked Kate.

'You'll see,' said Dad. 'You'll find out.'

'Another surprise,' said Kate.

'There's more!' said Dad. 'Two more to be exact. Now, Mum and I'll go and get the maps. You and Luke stay with Tom and make sure he doesn't wander off. Where is Luke?'

Luke was sitting in the car. Kate could see him; his head was down. He'd be scribbling in his notebook again.

'He was just getting the last of his things,' said Eve quickly.

Dad frowned. 'He's never there when you want him.'

Kate watched them go over to the
car and speak to Luke before they
went into the farmhouse. Luke didn't
get out of the car.

Kate held Tom's bridle and talked to
him, stroking his soft muzzle,
reaching up to pat his enormous neck.
She couldn't reach his ears. He was a
giant of a horse.

Suddenly he shifted his position.

He moved forwards, only a couple of steps, but Kate couldn't stop him.

'Luke!' screamed Kate. 'Help me!'

By the time Luke reached her, Tom had stopped.

'He can't move far,' said Luke. 'The brake's on.'

'Don't leave me,' said Kate. 'How do you know the brake's on?'

'I put it on,' said Luke. He disappeared into the caravan with his belongings.

Kate waved to Dad and Eve as they came out of the farmhouse. 'Are you coming now?' she called.

'Just going to park the car at the back,' called Dad.

When he and Eve reappeared, Dad was carrying a long thin parcel.

'Is that for me?' Kate said, when they arrived at the caravan.

'No,' said her father. 'This is for Luke. Where is he?'

'Inside,' said Kate, and followed them in.

'Here you are, Luke. Just a little surprise for the holiday,' said Dad.

'More a long, thin surprise,' said Eve.

Luke took the wrapping paper off and revealed a brand-new fishing-rod, with reel and line and spinners.

There was a silence.

'Thank you,' said Luke.

'All you need is bait,' said Dad. 'Everything else is there.'

'Thank you,' said Luke again, but he made no move to touch the fishing-rod.

'Don't you like it? said Dad. 'It'll give you something to do.'

'I already have something to do,' said Luke.

'Yes, but fishing's a sport,' said Dad. 'I used to love fishing when I was a boy.'

Luke began to pack the fishing-rod away.

'Well, I am surprised,' said Dad. 'I thought he'd be really pleased,' he said to Eve.

'I'm sure he will be,' said Eve, 'when he gives it a try.' Her eyes pleaded with Luke to make an effort. 'I'm hoping he'll teach me.'

Kate had heard enough about fishing. 'What about my surprise?' she said.

'Right,' said Dad. 'Well, we know Kate's is all right, don't we, love?' Eve smiled.

'You stay here,' said Dad. 'I'll fetch it.'

'Can't I come?' said Kate.

'No,' said her father. 'And don't look until I say so.'

Kate sat on the long seat, opening and shutting her eyes. 'Is he coming yet?' she kept asking. Then she thought she heard something. Surely . . . surely . . .

'He's here,' said Eve. 'You can come and look now.'

Kate sprang to the door.

Outside stood her father, and beside him stood a pony.

Kate leapt down the steps.

'Is he for me?' she said.

'Well, he's certainly not for me,' said her father, smiling. 'What do you think of him?'

Kate walked all round the pony. His coat was long and shaggy.

'What's his name?' she said.

'Blanco,' said Dad. 'Because he's white.'

'You don't have white ponies, Dad. White ponies are called grey.'

'Well, whatever he is, he's yours!' said Dad.

'How will we get him home?' said Kate. 'On the boat?'

'He's not going home,' said Dad.

Kate didn't understand. 'But you said he was mine.'

'He is yours,' said Dad. 'For the holiday. To ride whenever you want to. He's all yours for a whole week.'

Kate couldn't believe it. To be given a pony and then not to be given a pony.

'I don't want him for a week,' she said. 'I want him for always.' She was close to tears.

'Now you're being silly,' said her father. 'I thought you'd be pleased.'

Eve came quickly down the steps and put her arms round Kate. 'You're just tired,' she said. 'Tomorrow we'll saddle him up and ride him. We'll hitch him to the back today. It's time we were off, Paul.'

Kate pulled herself free and threw the end of the halter at Eve. Blanco's head shot up in alarm.

'I don't want to ride him tomorrow. I want to ride him for always. I told Sharon I was having a pony for ever.'

'Then you were very silly,' said her father.

'You told me a lie,' sobbed Kate. 'You told me I was having a pony of my own. You promised.'

Without another word, her father took the pony to the back of the caravan and tied him to a spare hook. Suddenly he looked very tired. It had been a long journey from the boat and he wanted to travel at least a couple of miles before they camped for the night.

'Don't worry,' said Eve, as he gathered up the reins. 'We're all very tired. Things are bound to be better in the morning.'

# 3. *Travelling*

Over the next few days things did get
better. The sun shone, making them
all feel more cheerful and, during the
day, as they travelled along, everyone
felt the benefit of being out in the
fresh air.

Dad or Eve handled the driving. Kate often rode the pony and one of them always walked at Tom's head. Though he was strong and could easily pull the caravan along the flat, straight roads, he was apt to stop suddenly for a snatch of grass. It was then that a friendly voice at his ear and encouragement in front as well as behind kept him going.

Walking at Tom's head was Kate's second favourite job. Although riding Blanco, which was the best thing, was hardly a job. Blanco was so friendly. He stood patiently while Kate groomed him; he stood quietly while the saddle and bridle were put on; he stood still while Kate mounted. He didn't always go in the direction Kate wanted him to. But she was learning to sit still in the saddle and keep her hands steady and wait until he had stopped twisting about, then, gently, urge him forwards. When Kate wasn't riding him, he trotted along happily behind the caravan.

The one thing that Blanco didn't like was leaving Tom. When they had stopped for the day and Kate wanted to go for a ride, Blanco hated leaving Tom behind. Sometimes Kate had to lead him away on foot, then, when she judged they were far enough away, mount and off they would go. Blanco was no trouble then.

Luke took his turn at Tom's head. But he didn't accept Kate's offer of a ride on Blanco and no one asked him if he'd like to drive.

The fishing-rod lay untouched on his bunk.

'Dad would show you how to use

it,' his mother said one night. 'You only have to ask.'

'If he wants to use it,' said Luke, 'he can.'

Kate would have liked to have a go at fishing but she didn't like to ask. Besides, most of the time she was too busy riding Blanco or looking after him.

Luke spent most of his time in the caravan, when it wasn't on the move. One day, when Eve and Dad went shopping to a nearby village, Kate came back from a ride and found Luke in the caravan with masses of paper all over the table. He was annoyed at being interrupted. Kate said if he told her what he was doing, she would go away again. Writing music, he said, well, not exactly writing it, arranging it. Copying out the parts for a band to play.

Kate only half understood what he meant, but she understood that it was important to him.

On the third day they reached the sea. Kate, at Tom's head, could smell the sea; she could hear the waves breaking on the pebbly shore; and every now and then, when Tom's head moved up out of the way, she caught a glimpse of the silvery-blueness of it beyond the stone wall at the side of the road. Soon, she told Tom, they would be camping by the sea.

'Kate! Wake up! We're stopping!' Her father was driving.

Kate stood out of the way while he steered Tom off the road. Each day they had to find a good, flat piece of ground so that the caravan was level and they wouldn't tip out of their bunks! There had to be a tap close by for water, both for themselves and the horses, and there had to be a good stretch of ground near the caravan for the horses to graze on. Each night they tethered Tom and Blanco on a good long rope so that they had plenty of freedom.

The first night they had stopped she had asked Dad where the toilet was.

Dad had pointed to the spade.

At first she didn't know what he meant and when she did, she couldn't believe it! But it was surprising what you could do when you had to, and now she was quite used to one or other of them disappearing over the horizon to find a suitable place to dig a hole!

'I thought we'd go down to the sea first today,' said Dad, as they unharnessed Tom.

Even Luke went with them. He had a contest with Dad as to who could throw a pebble the furthest and though Dad won, Luke was much better at skimming. He could make a flat pebble bounce across the waves three or four times before it sank into the water. He showed Kate how to do it, how to hold the flattest pebble you

could find with the tips of your fingers
and then throw it sort of sideways,
quickly. Every time Kate tried, the
pebble plopped into the water as soon
as it touched it.

'I'm going to get Blanco,' she
announced, after yet another pebble
had disappeared without trace into
the Atlantic Ocean.

When she came back Luke was
sitting alone, aiming at a rock.

'They've gone to the village,' he said.
'Mum said they wouldn't be long.'

Kate rode nearer to the sea. The beach was sandy there, now that the tide was going out. Kate would have liked to have ridden straight into the waves, like a girl in a book that she had once read. Her pony had swum into the sea with the girl on his back, riding the waves with him. But Blanco had his saddle on and, besides, he didn't seem too keen on actually going into the water.

So Kate rode along the beach. Blanco needed no urging. He was off like the wind. They galloped right to the end of the bay and back again. Kate felt that they were flying along. When she came back to Luke, she said: 'Aren't you doing your music today?'

'No,' he said. 'Not yet. I'm at a difficult bit. I'm thinking about it.'

'Would you like a ride?' said Kate.

'No, thanks!' said Luke. 'I think I'll stick to music. It's easier to control.'

He watched Kate canter off along the sands. When she came back he said: 'I'm off now. See you later.'

'I'll come too,' said Kate.

'You don't have to,' he said.

'Don't worry,' said Kate. 'I'm not

going to bother you. I just want to groom Blanco. That's all!'

Luke walked by the side of them as they went up the hill. Blanco was quieter, now that they were leaving the noise of the sea behind.

'Why don't you save up for a pony?' said Luke. 'If you really want one.'

'I couldn't,' said Kate.

The truth was she'd never really thought about the cost of a pony. She'd always wanted one, ever since she'd started lessons. She'd asked her father more than once.

'You could,' said Luke, 'if you put your mind to it.' He grinned up at her. 'That's what my gran says anyway – "Nothing's impossible if you put your mind to it."'

'But I don't have any money,' said Kate.

44

'What about pocket money?'

'Well, I spend it.'

Luke was impatient. 'What on?' he said. 'Sweets? Comics? You can do without those. Look. Is a pony something you want more than anything else in the world?'

'Yes,' said Kate immediately.

'Then start saving,' said Luke. 'What about Christmas and birthday money? What do you do with that?'

'Spend it,' said Kate.

'What on?' said Luke.

Kate couldn't remember. She simply couldn't remember.

'You could have saved it,' said Luke. 'By now you'd be a long way towards a pony. And if you saved up some money yourself, I bet your Dad would help you.'

'How do you know so much about

it?' said Kate. 'You don't own a pony.'

'No,' said Luke. 'But I own a piano.'

Kate remembered the piano arriving from Luke's house with all the other things. She hadn't known it was Luke's own.

'You could do a paper round,' said Luke.

'I couldn't,' said Kate. 'I'm not old enough.'

'You will be,' said Luke. 'You can do jobs for people. That's how I started. Cleaning cars. Things like that. It's surprising how it mounts up.'

'How long did it take you?' said Kate. The thought of saving all her pocket money, and Christmas and birthday money, horrified her.

'Two years,' said Luke.

It seemed a lifetime to Kate. She'd never do it.

As they turned into the field, she saw Eve and Dad at the caravan. She urged Blanco into a canter. 'I galloped right along the bay!' she shouted.

'Did you indeed?' said Dad. 'Well, we've found a pub that does terrific food. So it's out on the town tonight!'

One old man in the pub was very interested in their travels. Dad was glad he had brought the maps with him. 'We're crossing over to this island tomorrow,' he said. He showed the old man the route they would be taking.

'Never,' said the old man. 'That's too far. You'll be quicker going over the bay. Just here.' His finger jabbed the place on the map. He thought for a moment. 'The tide'll be out until late afternoon. You'll have all day to cross.'

'Over the sands!' said Kate. 'I can't wait!'

'I haven't said we're doing it yet,' said Dad. 'Are you sure it's safe?' he asked the man.

'Safe as houses,' he said. 'Cars go across all the time. My brother now, he never goes round by the road. He waits for the tide to go out, then over he goes. Minutes it takes. Ask anyone.'

Dad did. He asked the barman, who assured him that the sand was quite firm. Cars, even tractors, went backwards and forwards often.

'Let's do it, Dad!' said Kate.

'There's quite a way to go before we reach the bay,' said Dad. 'It'll mean an early start.'

# 4. *Ride to the rescue*

The next morning Kate, who was up first, stepped out to say good morning to Blanco. But there was no sign of Tom or Blanco anywhere. Kate felt her stomach sink. Tom had pulled the tethering hook out before but he'd never moved far away from Blanco. Now there was no sign of either of them. They could be anywhere. There were no gates or hedges to keep them in, just the heathland stretching away in every direction.

Kate felt sick. Now how would they make an early start? She went back into the caravan to break the news.

Her father said little, except to ask Luke if he was sure he had tethered the horses properly the night before.

'You know I did,' said Luke quietly. 'You came and checked. You always do.'

'Tom's pulled his hook out before,' said Kate.

While Eve began to cook the breakfast, she, Dad and Luke set off in different directions.

'Be back in half an hour,' said Dad, 'even if you haven't found them, and if you see anyone, ask.'

Kate walked back along the road they had travelled the day before. She saw no one and there was no sign of the horses. When she reached the village and checked her watch, she knew she had to turn back. She was tired and miserable and very hungry.

51

Yet, when she arrived back at the caravan and Eve put her breakfast in front of her, she couldn't eat any of it.

Dad ate his, repeatedly checking his watch. Luke had not returned.

Even when, an hour later, Luke did return and he was leading Tom and Blanco, Kate knew that by the time they had harnessed Tom and packed everything securely into the caravan, it would be a much later start than Dad had intended. They'd never get to the bay in time now.

52

Nobody talked much as they set off. Dad was driving.

Kate climbed up beside him. After a while she said, 'Are we going across the sands?'

'If there's time.'

'We'll have to,' said Eve, who was at Tom's head. 'We won't have time to go round by the road. We'd never make it before dark.'

'If the tide's on the turn,' said Dad, 'we'll have to go by road.'

'How can a road go to an island?' said Kate.

'It's a bridge,' her father said shortly.

Kate didn't ask any more. She wasn't interested in a bridge anyway. She wanted to go over the sands.

They didn't stop for lunch. Dad said they had to keep going.

Kate wished she had put Blanco's saddle and bridle on before they'd set off. She'd planned to do it when they stopped for lunch. She wanted to ride him across the sand. Her chance came when they reached the crossing place. Dad pulled up at the top of the slope which led down to the beach.

'The tide's well out,' said Luke.

'Look!' said Eve. 'You can see the island. It's not far.'

'Where?' said Kate. 'Let's see!' She

led Blanco to the front of the caravan.

The island looked very close. Cliffs rose steeply from the sea. But there was a break in the cliffs, a flat part, the way on to the island.

'He did say we were all right until late afternoon,' said Eve. 'That man in the pub.'

'I'd have been happier just to ask someone,' said Dad.

But there was no one in sight.

'You did ask someone,' said Luke.

'We ought to go if we're going,' said Eve.

'Cars and tractors go across,' said Luke.

Dad ignored them. He walked down the slipway to the beach. When he came back, he said: 'Right. You lead then, Eve. Luke, you come up with me. Kate –'

'I'm riding, Dad,' said Kate, mounting quickly.

'Right,' said Dad.

'Wagons roll!' Kate yelled, and set off at a fast trot down the slope, quite forgetting to tighten the girth beneath the saddle as she usually did.

'You keep your mind on what you're doing,' said Dad, as the caravan rumbled down the cobbled slope on to the beach. Tom stepped out on to the firm sand calmly, with no hesitation and continued at his usual steady pace. But Blanco was excited by the smell of the sea and the softer ground beneath his feet. He danced about on the sand.

'See you!' said Kate and urged him on. But Blanco, as usual, did not want to leave Tom. So Kate held him back until the caravan was a good way ahead and then off they went like the wind.

'This is fantastic!' she yelled as they drew level. She tried to urge Blanco on, to pass them, but he twisted and turned and wouldn't go on ahead. So Kate trotted around the caravan and beside it.

'Keep away from Tom!' shouted her father. 'You're in the way!'

So Kate held him back again. Blanco didn't like it. But Kate kept him on a tight rein and as soon as she gave him his head, he was off. Kate thought she had never been so happy.

Suddenly, just as they were almost level with the caravan again, Kate felt the saddle slip. She tried to push her foot firmly down in the right stirrup to bring it level again. But the saddle had slipped too far. Kate felt herself

falling. Blanco banged into Tom. Kate couldn't control him.

'Get out of the way!' shouted her father.

Kate screamed: 'I'm falling!'

Eve saw what was happening and rushed to Blanco's head to bring him to a standstill. The saddle had slipped so far over that Kate was able to fall safely to the ground.

'I couldn't help it,' said Kate, picking herself up. 'The saddle started slipping and I couldn't stop it.'

58

Eve quietened Blanco. Then she looked at the saddle.

'The girth's loose,' she said. 'Didn't you tighten it?'

Miserably, Kate shook her head. Eve undid the girth, put the saddle back in its proper place and pulled the girth up securely.

She gave Kate a hug. 'Don't worry,' she said. 'You'll be all right now. I'll give you a leg up.'

'I'll lead him for a bit,' said Kate. She was still shaking.

Eve was about to argue, when they heard Dad shout.

'Eve! For heaven's sake – where are you?'

The caravan, only a little way in front of them, had stopped.

Eve and Kate ran. As they reached the caravan, they saw that Tom had stopped to drink at a stream that was making its way to the sea. Dad was shouting at him to move on and slapping the reins on his back. Luke was trying to pull Tom's head up out of the water.

'I told you not to leave his head!' Dad shouted at her. 'He won't budge.'

'He can't budge,' said Eve. 'You'd better come down and look.'

Dad threw the reins on to Tom's back and jumped down.

'What are you on about?' he said. And then he saw what Eve had already seen.

The caravan's wheels had sunk into the sand. The lower rim of the wheels was completely hidden.

The caravan was stuck.

'We'll all have to push,' said Dad. 'Leave his head, Luke. All of us at the back.'

The three of them set their weight to the back of the caravan and pushed. Kate couldn't help because she was hanging on to Blanco and even if she had, her weight would have counted as nothing. It was no good. The wheels would begin to move, but as soon as Tom felt the weight of the caravan he stopped pulling, and the caravan rocked back into its groove. With each rock backwards, the wheels sank deeper into the sand.

'You go to the front, Kate,' said Dad. 'You pull Tom's head while we push.'

'What about Blanco?'

'Get on him!' said Dad. He took hold of her and hoisted her into the saddle. But though Kate kept urging him fowards, Blanco wouldn't go near Tom's head. He kept shying away from the pool of water.

'For goodness' sake, get a hold of him,' shouted Dad.

'I am trying,' said Kate. Blanco was twisting and turning, spraying up showers of water. Kate held the reins with one hand and reached for Tom's head with the other. When Blanco swung away to the side, Kate stayed with him, and then tried again and again.

It was Luke who noticed that the tide was coming in. Where there had been dry firm sand, there was now a covering of water.

'We could get the mats out of the caravan,' said Luke. 'If we put them in front of the wheels and Tom did move, the wheels would have something to grip on.'

Dad said nothing. He just stood at

the side, looking at the caravan. 'Right,' he said, after what seemed a very long time. 'We're not strong enough to push so we'll have to try coaxing Tom forwards. Luke, you get up and keep hold of the reins. Eve, you and I'll go to Tom's head and see if we can get him to move. Kate, you keep Blanco just ahead of us so that Tom will follow him.'

Twice Tom looked as if he was going to make a move, but again, as soon as he felt the caravan's weight behind him, he stopped.

'It's too much for him,' said Dad. 'It's in too deep.'

'What are we going to do?' said Kate.

'Tractors cross over here,' said Luke. 'A tractor could pull us out.'

Dad looked at Luke, then turned to

Kate. Blanco was becoming even more restless now his hoofs were under water. 'Kate, ride as quickly as you can to the island. Find help. Stop at the first farm.'

'Not on my own,' said Kate.

'I'll go,' said Luke.

'You can't,' said Dad. 'Kate'll be quicker riding and I need you here. We'll try your mats idea, then we'll push and Mum can pull. We've got to keep trying. Go on, Kate.'

'He won't go,' said Kate. 'He won't leave Tom. You know he won't.'

'You're not trying,' shouted her father. 'Do what you usually do. Get off and lead him for a bit.'

'I won't be able to get on again,' said Kate. She was frightened the saddle might slip.

'I'll go,' said Eve.

'No,' Dad shouted. 'I need you here.'

Luke went to Blanco's head. 'I'll lead him away for her,' he said, 'then I'll come back.'

He set off at a run. The sea was now up to his ankles. Blanco trotted with him. When he was far enough, he stopped.

'You'll be all right,' said Luke. 'Just do what your Dad says. Stop at the first farm and ask for help. Ask them to bring a tractor if they can.'

Kate said nothing.

'Look,' said Luke. 'You can do anything if you really want to.'

Still Kate sat. She knew she was no help at the caravan. She and Blanco just got in the way. And Kate wanted to help; she wanted the caravan to be out of the water and on to the island,

and all of them to be safe and happy
and everything just as it was before
this horrible day had started.

Kate made up her mind.

She turned Blanco's head and set off
at a canter towards the island.

# 5. *On the island*

At the first cottage she came to Kate
stopped. It wasn't a farm but whoever
lived there could tell her where the
nearest farm was, she thought. She
jumped off Blanco at the gate, ran
with him up the front path and
hammered on the front door.

There was no answer.

She knocked on the door again.
'Please come. Please come,' she
whispered to herself.

The silence that greeted her, as her
hand fell away from the door, was
frightening. A sudden gust of wind
blew loose grit around her feet. Blanco

stepped back in alarm. The sky had darkened and as Kate ran back down the path, the first spots of rain fell.

At the gate she mounted quickly and set off along the road. She had seen a house right at the top of the hill. If she could find the road up to it, she'd try there next.

She came to a steep track leading upwards. It was hardly a road, just a cart-track, but Kate noticed there were marks of tractor-wheels in the mud. Her heart lifted. A tractor could pull the caravan out of the sand.

At the top of the track was the house she had caught sight of. A square-built farmhouse and in the yard was a tractor. Kate jumped off Blanco and ran with him to a side-door. She hammered on it with all her strength. She willed it to open.

An old lady, dressed all in black, opened the door. A dark passage stretched behind her.

'I'd like to speak to the farmer,' Kate said. 'Please,' she said. 'We need help.'

The old lady looked at her. 'There's no one here,' she said.

Kate tried again.

The old lady didn't seem to understand. She pulled the black shawl closer.

'There's no one on the island,' she said.

Kate backed away. She was shivering. The rain had brought with it an early darkness and a bitter wind. Standing there on the hilltop, Kate felt chilled to the bone.

She clutched the reins in one hand and pulled herself into the saddle. 'Thank you,' she said. 'I'll try

somewhere else.'

'You'll find no one,' the old lady called after her. 'They've all gone to the mainland.'

As soon as she reached the track, Kate brought Blanco to a standstill. She looked around to see if there was another house she could try. But there was none.

Far below, she could just make out the caravan. It was too dark, and the fine, misty drizzle made it impossible to see anything clearly, but Kate knew that by now the sea would be well in. It had been swirling around the caravan when she had left and the deeper the water became, the more difficult it would be to get the caravan to move. What would they do? Dad wouldn't leave Tom. That was certain and it was equally certain that he would try to send Eve and Luke to safety – but even as Kate thought it, she knew they wouldn't go – and all the time the sea would be coming in – nothing could stop that.

Kate kicked Blanco into action. She had to keep trying. She had to get help. She was the one they were depending on.

She rode right round the farmhouse to the back. Perhaps there was another track there, leading to another farm.

There was nothing. Only barns and sheds and behind them fields and more fields.

Kate came back to the front of the farm and, as she did so, heard the noise of a car. She couldn't see it. The road curved away into the distance out of sight – but she could hear it.

The sound of it grew louder – and then Kate saw it – a small black car coming along the road.

Kate urged Blanco on. The rain had stopped but the cold wind stung her cheeks and made her eyes stream as she hurtled down the steep path. She remembered to lean back in the saddle and ease the reins to help Blanco keep his footing and she found herself shouting, shouting . . .

When she reached the bottom of the track, the car was disappearing into the distance.

Kate stood up in the stirrups, shouting, waving. But the car showed no signs of stopping. Kate urged Blanco after it but knew after a few yards that it was useless. The car had gone. The road lay empty in front of her.

Kate pulled Blanco up. She tried to think. If she carried on following the car, going in the direction it had taken, it could have stopped by now.

But she couldn't be sure. It could be miles away.

She turned Blanco and set off at a gallop in the opposite direction, past the track she had just come down, going in the direction from which the car had come. Surely the old lady was wrong – there must be someone on the island.

The road twisted and turned and Kate slowed to a trot. It was too dangerous to go so fast. If another car came round a corner too quickly . . . another car . . . Kate seized on the thought. If there had been one car, there could be another. Just then, she saw one. The road had straightened out and, as yet, the car was only a speck in the distance, but it was coming this way, coming towards her. She pulled Blanco over to the side of the road.

The car was coming. Blanco wouldn't keep still. The car was getting nearer. Blanco pulled at the reins and tried to twist round. The car mustn't pass. This time it mustn't pass. Kate urged Blanco into the middle of the road and kept him there.

The car pulled up a few yards away from her.

'What do you think you're doing?' the driver shouted at her.

'I need help,' cried Kate. She rode up to the car. Inside were the driver and three other people. Surely they would help. Quickly she poured out the story.

'Right,' said the driver. 'You lead the way. We'll follow.'

Where the road ended they parked the car and, bringing with them some strong ropes and taking no notice of the water lapping over their feet, hurried with Kate to the caravan.

Luke and Dad were beginning to lift things out. 'We thought we'd have to leave it,' Dad explained. 'We were just about to unharness Tom and get him to safety.'

He told the newcomers what they had already tried to do and how they couldn't get Tom to keep going.

'Let's see what a bit of extra weight will do,' said one of the men.

'Right,' said Dad. 'Eve, you go to his head. The rest of us will push. Kate, you keep Blanco just in front of Tom.' He saw that she was shivering. 'Are you all right?' he said.

'I'm cold,' said Kate. Now that she was back at the caravan, now that the rescue no longer depended on her alone, she felt dizzy and very tired. She couldn't stop shivering. Her father took off his jumper and pulled it over her head. 'There,' he said, 'that'll help. You're a heroine,' he whispered, 'do you know that?'

Then everyone, except Kate and Blanco and Eve, went to the back of

the caravan and pushed. They didn't
need the ropes because at the second
heave Tom was able to move.
Everyone kept pushing and Tom
strained forwards and Eve shouted in
his ear, 'Come on, Tom, you can do it,
you can do it,' and Dad shouted,
'Keep pushing, keep pushing, it's

moving, it's moving,' and the caravan came out of the sand with a sickening, sudden squelch. Tom nearly knocked Eve over as he swung to one side.

'Keep him going!' shouted Dad. 'Luke, jump up and steer him. I'll help Mum.'

And so, with Luke driving, Kate and Blanco leading and everyone else following on behind, pushing, they all came safely to the island.

Dad thanked their helpers and walked with them to their car. They were out for the day, sightseeing, they told him, but they hadn't expected to see the sight they had seen!

When Dad came back, they unharnessed Tom and set up camp for the night. Eve made hot drinks for all of them, and Kate told them all about her ride on to the island.

Even when they had finished their meal that night, they were still talking about the afternoon's adventures. When Dad said they'd definitely go back by the road, no one argued.

'Weren't we lucky those people were visiting the island?' said Eve, for the umpteenth time.

'We're lucky we had such a good rescue rider,' said Dad. 'I'm really proud of you, Kate.'

'Luke helped me,' said Kate. 'He told me I could do it.'

'I'm proud of both of you,' said Dad. 'Luke, I think you'd better share the driving from now on. I don't think we'd be sitting here now if you hadn't kept Tom going.'

Luke began to wash the dishes. Dad picked up a tea-towel.

'You don't have to,' said Dad. 'It was just a thought.'

'I'd like to,' said Luke.

# 6. *Another promise*

On the first Saturday after they
arrived home, it was Kate's birthday.
Later in the day, Sharon was to come
for tea and then they were going
riding together, an extra ride, a
birthday treat. It had all been arranged
before the holiday. At the time Kate
had been looking forward to it, but
now Kate knew what Sharon would
ask the minute she arrived. It was not
going to be easy to explain about not
having a pony.

Through the door came letters and
cards and Kate pushed thoughts of
the coming afternoon out of her mind.

Inside some of the letters was money, with messages that said 'buy yourself a little something' or 'buy something of your choice'. Kate arranged the cards on the mantelpiece and put all the money into one of the envelopes. Then she opened her presents.

From Eve and Dad there was a yellow tie, with brown horses galloping across it, and a gold tie-pin in the shape of a horse.

'Thank you,' said Kate, giving them each a hug.

Luke gave her a small, flat parcel with his card. On the outside of the parcel was the word FRAGILE. Kate opened it carefully. Inside was a framed photograph of Blanco. He was standing by the caravan, his ears pricked, his shaggy mane blowing in the wind.

'I took it when you were off on that long walk with Mum and Dad,' Luke said. 'In fact, I took a few but I thought you'd like this one best.'

'It's lovely,' said Kate. 'It's perfect.' Tears came suddenly into her eyes. When the time had come to leave, the hardest part had been saying goodbye to Blanco. Perhaps it was then that she had made up her mind.

'I thought you might want to look at him now and then,' said Luke.

Kate placed the photograph on the table in front of her. 'I will,' she said. 'I'll keep it in my room. It's lovely.' She picked up the card to open it. Inside was a five-pound note.

'Luke!' said Kate. 'Thanks – I never expected . . .'

'You can do anything you like with it,' said Luke. 'You don't have to . . .'

'I know exactly what I'm going to do with it,' said Kate. She put it with the other money in the envelope. 'I'm going to save it!'

'All of it?' said Dad when, later that morning, he drove Kate into town to open her own savings account.

'All of it,' said Kate.

'Wouldn't you like to keep some of it to spend?' he said.

But Kate handed over all the birthday money.

'That's the start of my Pony Fund,' she said, as they drove home.

If Kate had ever imagined for one moment that a pony would appear on her birthday, she had come to realize it just wasn't possible. Dad had explained on holiday how sorry he was that she'd thought Blanco was for keeps; and he'd looked so miserable and upset about it that Kate had assured him that having a pony to look after for a whole week, to ride whenever she wanted to, was wonderful.

But inside herself, she knew it wasn't enough. Perhaps it was then that she had made up her mind.

'You're really serious then?' said Dad.

'Yes,' said Kate, and for the rest of the journey home Kate told him the plans she had for earning money to save. She told him about Luke and the piano.

'I know I can't do a paper round yet,' she said, 'but I can clean cars and windows and weed gardens and maybe someone will need their dog taking for a walk. There must be lots of things I can do.'

When Sharon arrived, even before Kate opened the present she had brought, she said: 'Are you? Are you having a pony?'

'No,' said Kate. 'Well . . .'

'You either are or you aren't,' said Sharon.

Kate showed her the photograph of Blanco. 'He was mine,' she said. 'He was my very own for a whole week.'

But Sharon had been hoping for news of a pony at home, one that she could ride as well as Kate. 'What good's a pony for a week?' she said.

The birthday tea was quiet and Kate was glad when it was time to go to the stables.

'Has Kate told you about her ride to the rescue?' said Dad.

'No,' said Sharon. So Dad did. Including the part about being very proud of her.

'Has she told you about her pony?'

'What pony?' said Sharon. 'That one on holiday?'

'No, not that one,' said Dad. He pulled into the car-park in front of the stables. 'The one she's saving up for,' he said, as they all got out of the car. 'The one we're going to help her with.'

'Are you?' said Kate.

'Oh, yes,' said Dad. 'Mum and I thought we would! We had a long chat this afternoon and I understand Luke could do with some help towards a keyboard, and you could do with some help towards a pony –'

'You don't have to,' said Kate quickly. 'I mean . . .'

'We'd like to,' said Dad firmly, as they walked down to the stables. 'If you're prepared to save we're prepared to help, and that's a promise. You know,' he said. 'Years ago, I started to save for a fishing-rod.'

'Did you ever get it?' said Kate.

'No,' said Dad. 'Not then. But I have now.' He grinned. 'A spanking new one. Well, second-hand, hardly used!'

'From Luke?' Kate guessed.

'Yes,' said Dad. 'Well, he did have a go, didn't he? But I can quite see he hasn't time for music, exams and fishing. So you see, miracles do happen. Dreams do come true!'

Kate hugged him. 'See you later, Dad,' she said.

Mrs Farmer was waiting for them inside the stables. They were the first to arrive for their ride. 'Take your pick,' she said.

'Tommy, please,' said Sharon at once.

'I'd like to try Rainbow,' said Kate.

'You're full of surprises!' grinned Sharon, as she slipped the bridle over Tommy's head. 'First you're not having a pony, then you are. Then, apparently, you were the heroine of the honeymoon, and now you're riding Rainbow!'

Later, as they were riding along, Sharon said, 'Kate, when you get your own pony . . .' Kate knew what was coming. She knew Sharon was going to ask if she could ride him too.

'When you get your own pony,' said Sharon again. She stopped. 'Will you let me . . .' She stopped again. 'What are you going to call him?' she said.

Into Kate's mind came a pony – black, jet-black, as black as coal, as black as midnight – midnight . . .

'When I get my own pony,' said Kate, 'you can ride him too, and we'll call him Midnight!'

Ahead of them the line of ponies trotted off the road and on to the grassy track that led up the side of the moor. At the front of the line, Mrs Farmer stood up in her stirrups and waved her arm high in the air.

'Prepare to canter!' she yelled.

Kate tightened her reins. Rainbow danced impatiently, jingling his bit, tossing his head in the air, side-stepping: he wanted to be off. But Kate knew the pony in front of her was too close for her to go yet. She kept her knees pressed close to the saddle and her hands still.

Riding Rainbow wasn't like riding Toffee, or even Blanco. Rainbow was on the move all the time:

every pony had different ways of behaving. When she had her own pony, Kate thought, she would have to get to know him, learn his different habits. They would get to know each other.

'Canter on!' yelled Mrs Farmer.

The pony in front was off now and Kate gave Rainbow his head. He was away up the hill like a rocket.

'Hang on!' yelled Sharon. 'Wait for me!'